A Hat for Gran

by Sue Graves and A. Corazon Abierto

W

D0434544

Gran looked in the mirror.
"This hat is too old," she said.

Gran went to the hat shop.
"I want a new hat," she said.

"I like this hat," said Gran.

But the hat was too big.

"I like this hat," said Gran.

But the hat was too small.

"I like this hat," said Gran.

But the hat was too tickly.

"I like this hat," said Gran.

But the hat was too furry!

Gran looked at the hats.

"I want a new hat," she said.

"Look at this hat," said Gran.

17

"I like this hat," said Gran.
"This is the hat for me."

19

Story trail

Start

Start at the beginning of the story trail. Ask your child to retell the story in their own words, pointing to each picture in turn to recall the sequence of events.

Independent Reading

This series is designed to provide an opportunity for your child to read on their own. These notes are written for you to help your child choose a book and to read it independently.

In school, your child's teacher will often be using reading books which have been banded to support the process of learning to read.

Use the book band colour your child is reading in school to help you make a good choice. *A Hat for Gran* is a good choice for children reading at Yellow Band in their classroom to read independently.

The aim of independent reading is to read this book with ease, so that your child enjoys the story and relates it to their own experiences.

About the book
Gran really needs a new hat as her old one is falling apart. She visits the hat shop and tries on lots of hats, but none of these new hats are quite right for her.

Before reading
Help your child to learn how to make good choices by asking: "Why did you choose this book? Why do you think you will enjoy it?" Look at the cover together and ask: "What do you think the story will be about?" Support your child to think of what they already know about the story context. Read the title aloud and ask: "Do you think Gran needs a new hat? Why do you think that?" Remind your child that they can try to sound out the letters to make a word if they get stuck.

Decide together whether your child will read the story independently or read it aloud to you. When books are short, as at Yellow Band, your child may wish to do both!

During reading

If reading aloud, support your child if they hesitate or ask for help by telling the word. Remind your child of what they know and what they can do independently.

If reading to themselves, remind your child that they can come and ask for your help if stuck.

After reading

Support comprehension by asking your child to tell you about the story. Use the story trail to encourage your child to retell the story in the right sequence, in their own words.

Give your child a chance to respond to the story: "Did you have a favourite part? Do you like going shopping? Do you have a favourite thing to wear even if it is a bit old or small for you?"

Help your child think about the messages in the book that go beyond the story and ask: "Do you think Gran and her grandchild had fun at the hat shop? Why / why not?"

Extending learning

Help your child understand the story structure by using the same sentence patterns and adding some new elements. "Let's make up a new story about Gran and something she needs to buy. 'This coat is too old,' said Gran. 'I like this coat!' said Gran. But the coat was too long. Now you try. What will Gran need to buy in your story?"

Your child's teacher will be talking about punctuation at Yellow Band. On a few of the pages, check your child can recognise capital letters, question marks, exclamation marks and full stops by asking them to point these out.

Franklin Watts
First published in Great Britain in 2019
by The Watts Publishing Group

Copyright © The Watts Publishing Group 2019

All rights reserved.

Series Editors: Jackie Hamley and Melanie Palmer
Series Advisors: Dr Sue Bodman and Glen Franklin
Series Designer: Peter Scoulding

A CIP catalogue record for this book is
available from the British Library.

ISBN 978 1 4451 6795 4 (hbk)
ISBN 978 1 4451 6797 8 (pbk)
ISBN 978 1 4451 6796 1 (library ebook)

Printed in China

Franklin Watts
An imprint of
Hachette Children's Group
Part of The Watts Publishing Group
Carmelite House
50 Victoria Embankment
London EC4Y 0DZ

An Hachette UK Company
www.hachette.co.uk

www.franklinwatts.co.uk

FSC
www.fsc.org
MIX
Paper from
responsible sources
FSC® C104740